Suraj manjunath revankar

First Published in October 2021

ISBN: 978-93-5472-286-8

BLUEROSE PUBLISHERS

www.bluerosepublishers.com

info@bluerosepublishers.com

+91 8882 898 898

Cover Design:

Shreya Kapoor

Typographic Design:

Namrata Saini

Distributed by: BlueRose, Amazon, Flipkart, Shopclues

Once upon a time, a place called Daanva was enjoying a pleasant atmosphere. It was under the control of Durvimochana and his wife Dushala. They used to nurture the people in a good manner and never harassed them for labour. But the only reason for their sorrow was that they didn't have a child to succeed the King .

प्रसाद विभाग
प्रसाद भंडार

One day, Durvimochana and his wife went to a temple to serve needy people, as they have been doing for many years. On that day, one saint was sitting with the needy people with a hungry stomach. When the King served food to that saint, the saint beca me happy and he immediately said to the King that he was happy with his kind nature and for that reason he would give him one boon. The king could use this boon at any time in his life. After listening to these words of the saint , Durvimochana thought about benefit of the Daanva region while Dushala thought about their children.

On the other hand Durvimochana said, "No, we should keep this boon and use it for Daanva in the case of a tough situation in future."

Dushala said, " If you will not use this boon to beget our children the n I will give up my life in your presence ." Listening to this he fell into a dilemma and was finally left with no choice.

He prayed to Brahmadev to bless them with children. Brahmadev accepted his prayers and was ready to bless him with children but before that he put forth two conditions:

First condition was that he should never interrupt while the war is going on and that he will not stop their children from continuing it. If he stopped them from fighting then they would easily die in the battle. Secondly, his sixth child will be born blind but he will have the power to replace his face with any ones.

Durvimochana was ready to accept any condition and that's why he said, “Yes, I am ready." After that Brahmadev blessed them with six children and went away. The King called the doorman and told him to spread the news that the king got a successor for the region of Daanva.

Now, he organized a grand celebration on the occasion of the naming ceremony of their children. He announced that at the age of 21 years, their children will be fit to go on the battle- field and conquer the opponent king in the war to gain victory. As a reward they can marry the princesses of the opponent king.

The names of the children were as follows :

1. Bhagirat - having power of Earth.
2. Varunesh - having power of Water.
3. Varadh - having power of Fire
4. Dishant - having power of Sky.
5. Anilesh - having power of Wind.
6. Nayanth - having power of Eyes.

Now, Nayanth was born blind. So Durvimochana and Dushala were too possessive of him. Due to this, the remaining children developed a feeling of hatred towards Nayanth. They used to trouble him to such an extent that he couldn't bear it. But he was not able to express it in front of parents . One day, after a few years had passed, all five children planned that they would carry Nayanth and leave him in the forest alone. According to their planning they left him in the forest and came back to the palace and pretended as if they didn't know anything about it. When Durvimochana came to know about Nayanth's disappearance , he immediately ordered the soldiers to find out where Nayanth was. But even after lots of efforts, they couldn't find Nayanth.

In the forest, Nayanth met a saint. The saint said that he knew Nayanth and asked how he had come here. Nayanth described all the incidents which took place in his life and further requested the saint to show him a way. The saint the n asked him to firstly close his eyes. He then covered Nayanth's eyes with a mus lin cloth and gave him one mantra, which he had to chant a few times. The mantra was: "Om Dristiyeh Namah." When Nayanth started chanting mantra, the saint made him invisible so that nobody could disturb him.

This was the reason why the soldiers couldn't find him, despite reaching that place, as he was invisible. As time passed on, many animals went over to Nayanth, but he didn't get injured.

After successfully completing his chanting process, Naynidevi manifested in front of him. She blessed him with eyes and said that Lord Shiva had been happy with his worship. Therefore, he was given one special power . She said that during his worship many animals went over him and that's why Lord Shiva said, " When you shoot your arrows towards another person, your arrows will be converted into animals which will fight with others."

After this, the saint ca me and said, "Nayanth, now you have to take another power and I will tell you how to get that. You have to stare at one tree continuously after I untie cloth from your eyes. You must look at it continuously until that tree catches fire." Nayanth followed the instructions without asking any questions.

After a while it caught fire. The saint said that in the war, when he drops the arrow in the middle of the ground at that time one transparent glass will appear. Through this glass, when an opponent will drop their arms over him, their arms will be reflected back to kill their own soldiers. This thing can be repeated only thrice in a war.

Nayanth asked the Saint what he should do next, and the saint replied, "This is something you should think over yourself. I cannot suggest anything ." After saying this, the saint went away and Nayanth was le ft thinking about the next step.

He decided that first he should go to the palace and continue to pretend there as if he were blind. After he entered the palace, his parents became happy and his brother s got disappointed. Even then his brother s continued to try to trouble him, but this time Nayanth easily managed to overcome their plans. In the mornings, the Guru ji would teach the five children the art of war, which included how to fight and the way to use weapons in war. Nayanth stood there and watched all their moves carefully and he practiced it at night.

Now all children reached the age of 21 years. King Durvimochana made the announcement, to all residents of Daanva, that their children would now be able to go on battle ground for war. He declared that after being victorious, his sons would marry the princesses of the defeated opponent king. All five children went to war and after winning the battle they came back with their brides.

The name s of the brides was :

- Suchitra

-Akshila

- Damayanthi

- Kanika

- Lathika

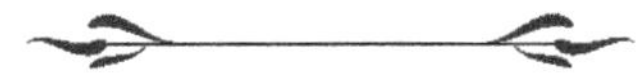

Their marriage was conducted. But before the first night of the married couples , Nayanth used his power and managed to replace his face with that of his brother s'; then he went to each bride's room, one by one, and planned to have a child from each of them. After nine months all five queens gave birth to one male child each.

Names as follows :

-Angad

- Dhruv

- Gaurav

- Indrajit

- Omkar

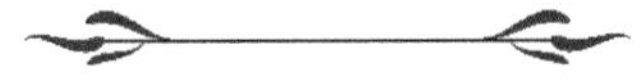

After some years Nayanth carried all his five son s away, to the forest. He trained them to fight and also taught them certain fighting skills. He made them wise warriors. Nayanth's main motto was to teach a lesson to all of his five brothers because they troubled him a lot. When all five of his sons were ready to step on to the battle- field, he brought them back to the palace . They had been away for a period of ten years, during which, in Durvimochana's palace, many successors were born. Their names were as follow :-

Bhagirat - Suchitra = Mahant (Boy)

=Aadrika(Girl)

Varunesh - Akhila = Badri (Boy)

= Naksh (Boy)

Varadh - Damayanti = Dakshita (Girl)

Dishant - Kanika = Balbir (Boy)

Anilesh - Lathika = Aashritha (Girl)

After reaching the palace, Nayanth challenged his brothers to fight a war against him and his son s. It was so that he could win the battle and teach a lesson. He also wanted to win the throne. According to his plans he brought them to the battle- field and the war began.

Now, the war had been dragged to the extreme level. Looking at the brutal war, Durvimochana got scared; he felt that whatever war was going on, in front of his eyes, was not right. So he decided to stop the battle. There fore, he ordered his son s to stop the battle at that mo ment itself. But, while he was taking this decision, he forgot what Brahma dev had kept as one condition (he was not to stop his son s during the war, at any moment, or else he would lose them). This was an advantage to Nayanth; he and his sons shot arrows at their opponents and unfortunately Durvimochana lost all his sons. Thus, Nayanth got justice for himself; further he received the throne of the kingdom of Daanva .

Durvimochana had beco me disheartened and Dushala ca me in front of him with tears in her eyes. She said, " We can't get our sons back anymore. Whatever the gods have written in our destiny will happen . We can't change it. But since our beloved child Nayanth has become the king of our kingdom, we should find bride for him." The news of searching for a bride for Nayanth, spread over the region. Some villagers came to Durvimochana to raise their voice against the marriage proposal. They reminded him that he had declared that when his son s would conquer the opponent king in the war, they would get to marry the princesses of that kingdom .

At this point Durvimochana fell in to a dilemma . Not understanding what he should do next, he finally decided to marry off his daughters- in- law to Nayanth. Listening to this decision, out of the five daughters- in- law , Suchitra was very disheartened. She planned to kill Nayanth by serving him food mixed with poison. She notified all her sisters- in- law of her plan. After this marriage occasion had taken place, Durvimochana sent all his grandsons to the *ashram*.

After the marriage , whenever Nayanth had to meet any of his wives, he used to replace his face with that of the respective husbands. He did so to make them feel com fortable and to help them lead a happier life.

One day all of the wives decided together to accept Nayanth as their husband. They went to Nayanth and said, "We have accepted the reality and we all of us also accept you as our husband. So you please don't camouflage yourself or im itate our husbands' faces."

Listening to these words, Nayanth's heart was filled with joy. But he had no knowledge of the big accident which was soon coming his way. Then days passed until one day, as he was having food, he fainted on the floor. Everyone was shocked to see such a thing happening. But they were not able to find the culprit.

Durvamochana called his soldier s and ordered them to find out who had committed such a criminal offence. He called a doctor, as well, to treat Nayanth immediately. The doctor declared that somebody had given poison to Nayanth. However, he relieved everyone by saying that he had cured him. By evening, the soldiers caught hold of the servant who had done this offence; they made him stand before the king.

The servant was asked to speak out the name of the person who had directed him to do this thing. At last he told that the name was ; 'Suchitra,' i.e. one of the daughters-in-law of Durvimochana. When everyone got to know that the name was revealed, the other daughters-in-law opened up. They informed the king that Suchitra was planning to kill Nayanth, since the very beginning of the marriage. Therefore, she directed one of the servants to poison the food and serve it to the king. Listening to this truth, Nayanth got aggrie ved and killed the servant. Following Nayanth's orders, Suchitra was immediately put behind the bars. But the story doesn't end here.

It was too late to understand that this was all done by Kanika and not Suchitra. It couldn't be understood as Kanika was behaving differently at that point.

After this, Nayanth organized for an offering of prayers to God in front of the fire. It was so that he could possess the eternal power of the universe and could never be further dethroned by any of the king or opponents. By this he could not only protect Daanva but also be the king of kings.

He didn't want any hurdles during the course of worship. He ordered his servants not to allow any one, not even his wives, to come to him, while he was engaged in that worship . In this way he continued to worship for twenty-one days. During this period he had to even undergo starvation.

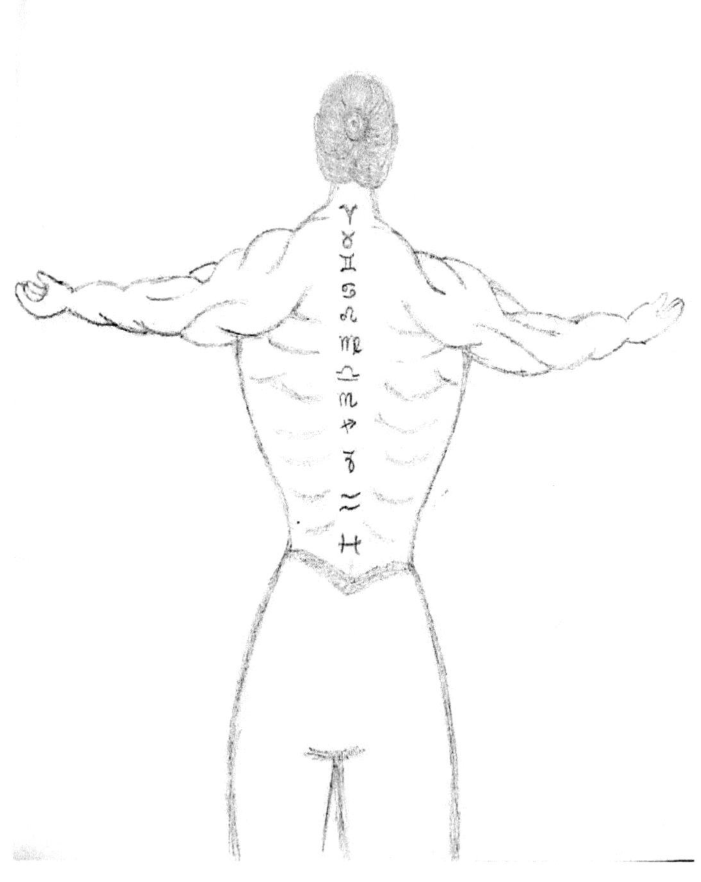

After the completion of this worship, he went to meet Suchitra, who had been imprisoned . He secretly told her that he already knew who the real culprit was. He said, "I know who tried to kill me but, at that situation, I was not in the position to reveal the name because it was not the right time."

The n Suchitra asked Nayanth, "Who was it ?"

He answered , "It was Kanika." He further informed her that he purposely didn't reveal her name because she carries a ring which can destroy the whole kingdom. So, in order to destroy that ring, he had arranged for this powerful worship through which he would be able to contain the power of the twelve zodiacs. He explained that she was trying to kill him because she wanted to take revenge for the loss of her husband. Therefore, she did all this collusion. He further told her, secretly, that he would now release her from jail. He assigned her a very important task: after he had entered into the ring Suchitra would need to remove that ring from Kanika's finger without her knowledge. As per plan, she tried to remove it, but there began a fight between Kanika and Suchitra. In that fight they lost the ring which held the precious stone. However, as Nayanth had already entered the ring, he lost his eternal power since the stone was lost from the ring. So he got restricted inside that stone itself, making it impossible for him to come out. While on other hand his eternal power of the twelve zodiacs came out as a human being.

To be continued.....

www.ingramcontent.com/pod-product-compliance
Ingram Content Group UK Ltd.
Pitfield, Milton Keynes, MK11 3LW, UK
UKHW021934190726
13853UKWH00004B/1430